Classics
⤳ to ⤲
Color

The Adventures of
Huckleberry
Finn

Racehorse for Young Readers books may be purchased in bulk at special discounts for sales promotion, corporate gifts, fund-raising, or educational purposes. Special editions can also be created to specifications. For details, contact the Special Sales Department, Skyhorse Publishing, 307 West 36th Street, 11th Floor, New York, NY 10018 or info@ skyhorsepublishing.com.

Racehorse for Young Readers™ is a pending trademark of Skyhorse Publishing, Inc.®, a Delaware corporation.

Visit our website at www.skyhorsepublishing.com.

10 9 8 7 6 5 4 3 2 1

Cover design by Brian Peterson
Cover and interior illustration by Diego Jourdan Pereira

ISBN: 978-1-944686-99-4

Printed in the United States of America

Classics to Color

The Adventures of Huckleberry Finn

FOR
YOUNG
READERS

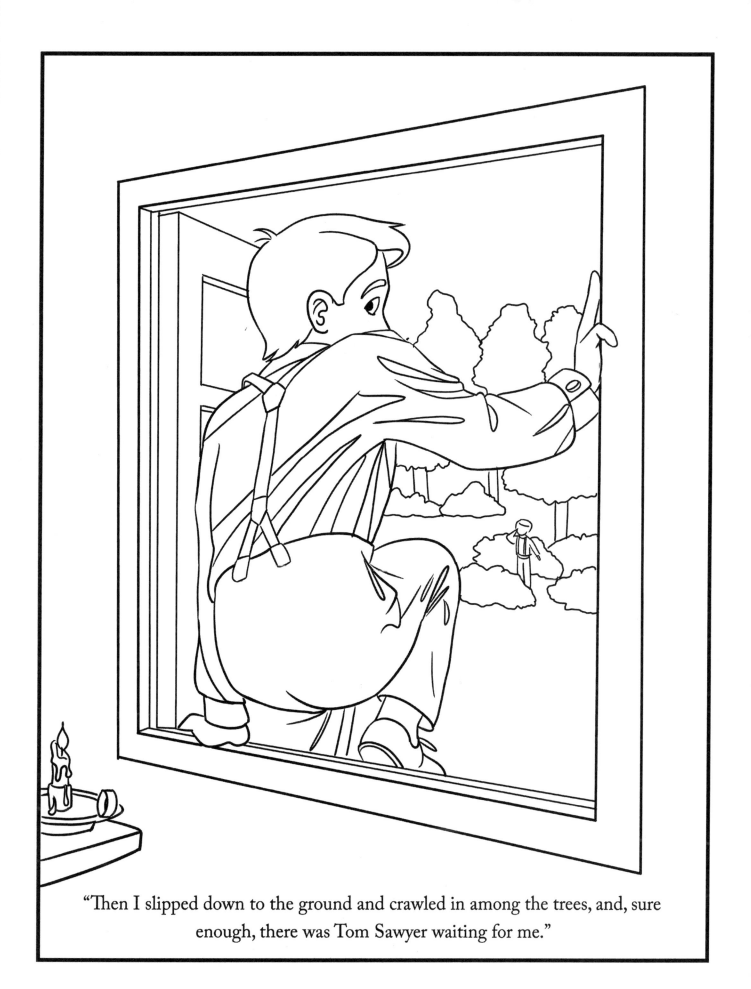

"Then I slipped down to the ground and crawled in among the trees, and, sure enough, there was Tom Sawyer waiting for me."

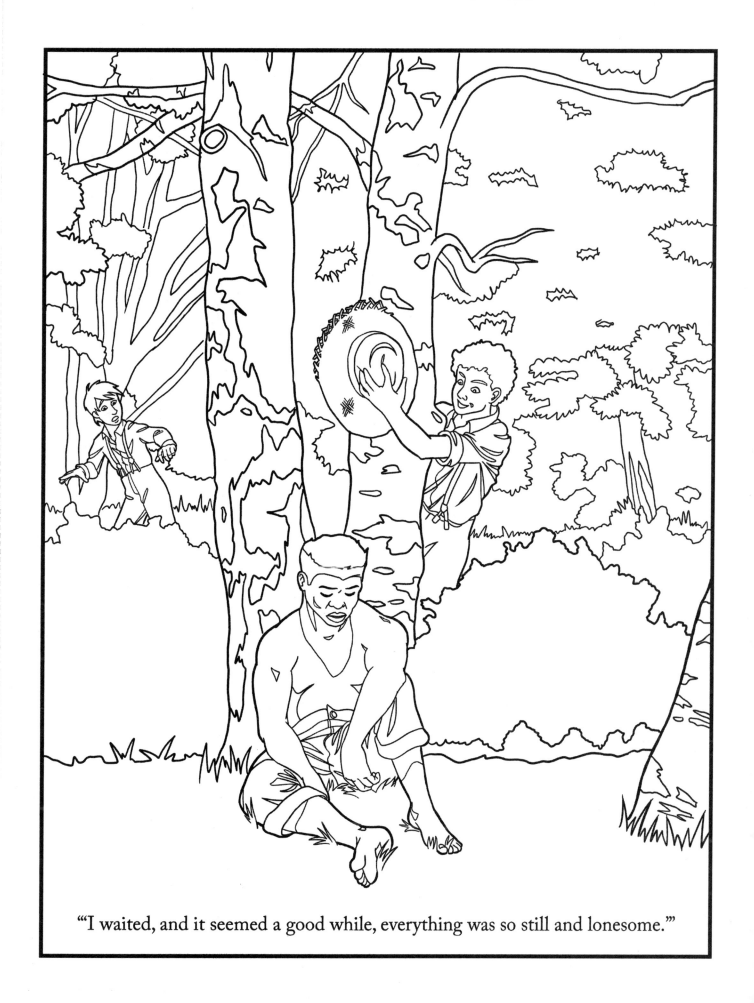

"'I waited, and it seemed a good while, everything was so still and lonesome.'"

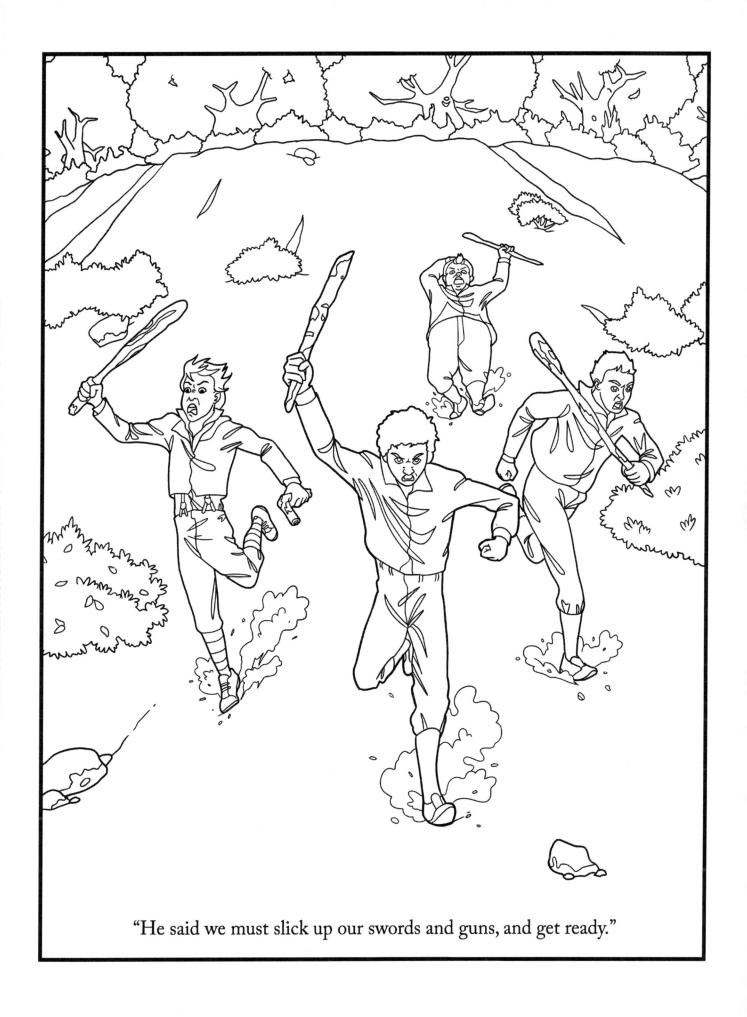

"He said we must slick up our swords and guns, and get ready."

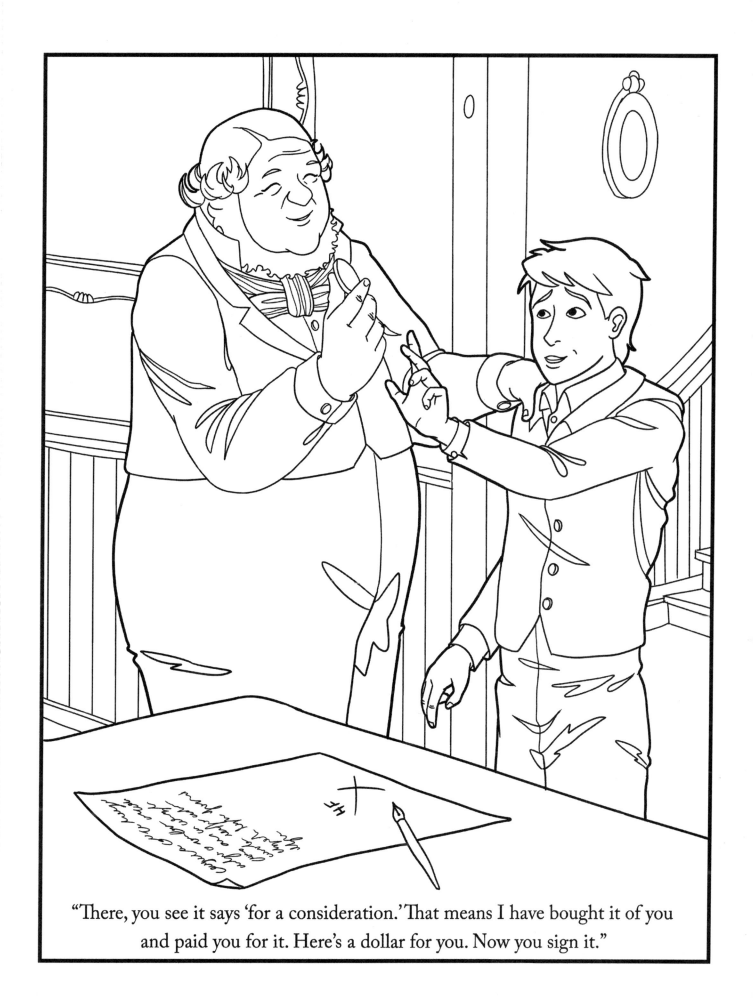

"There, you see it says 'for a consideration.' That means I have bought it of you and paid you for it. Here's a dollar for you. Now you sign it."

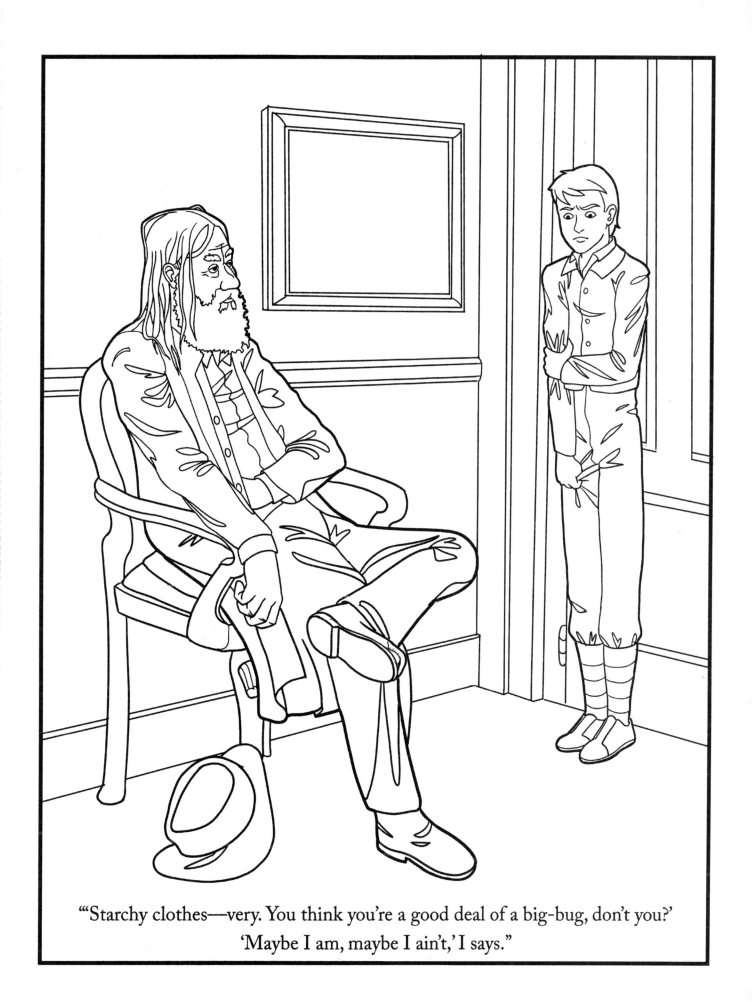

"'Starchy clothes—very. You think you're a good deal of a big-bug, don't you?'
'Maybe I am, maybe I ain't,' I says."

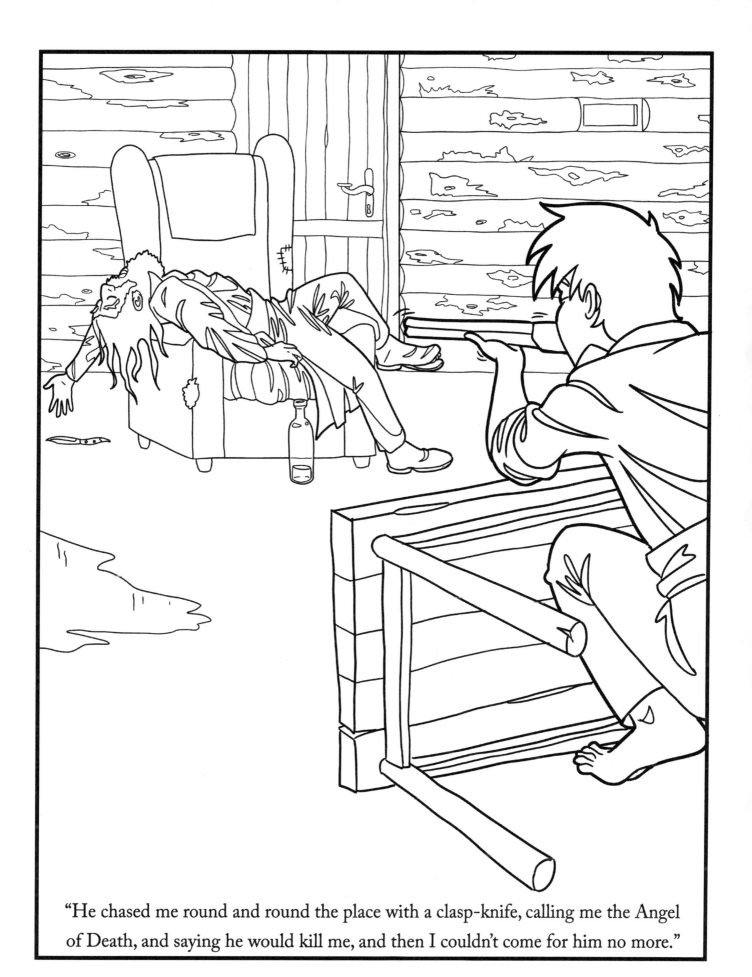

"He chased me round and round the place with a clasp-knife, calling me the Angel of Death, and saying he would kill me, and then I couldn't come for him no more."

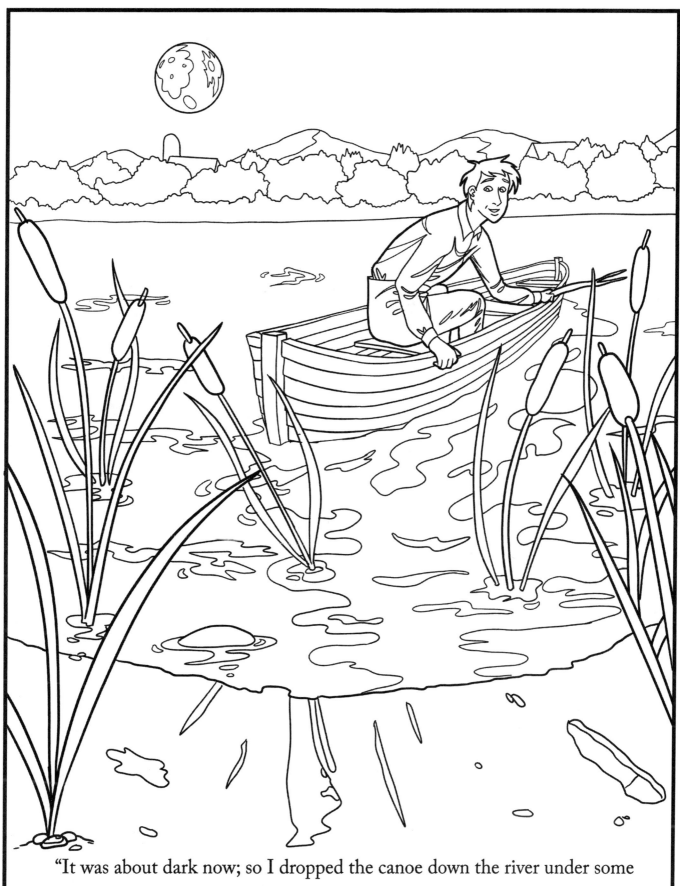

"It was about dark now; so I dropped the canoe down the river under some willows that hung over the bank, and waited for the moon to rise."

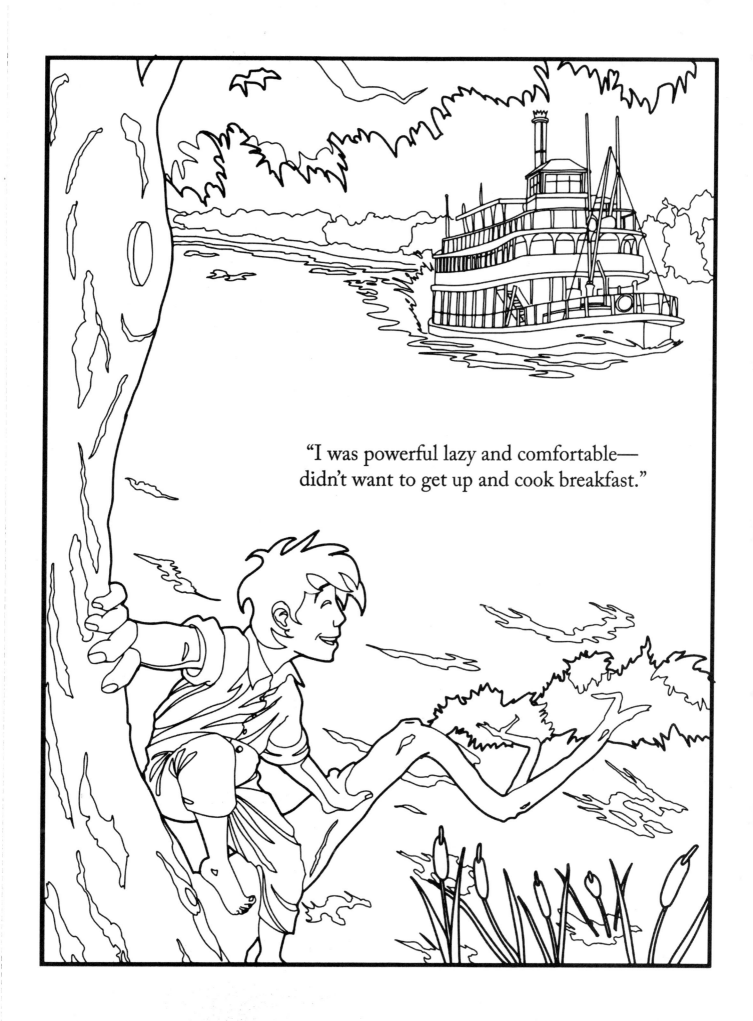

"I was powerful lazy and comfortable—
didn't want to get up and cook breakfast."

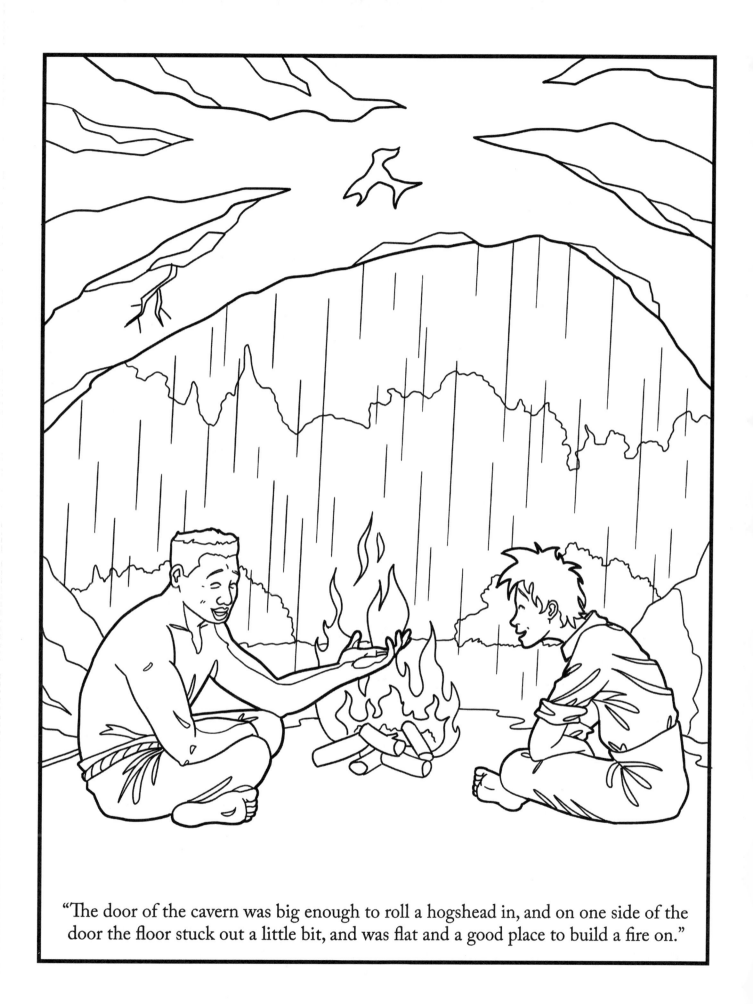

"The door of the cavern was big enough to roll a hogshead in, and on one side of the door the floor stuck out a little bit, and was flat and a good place to build a fire on."

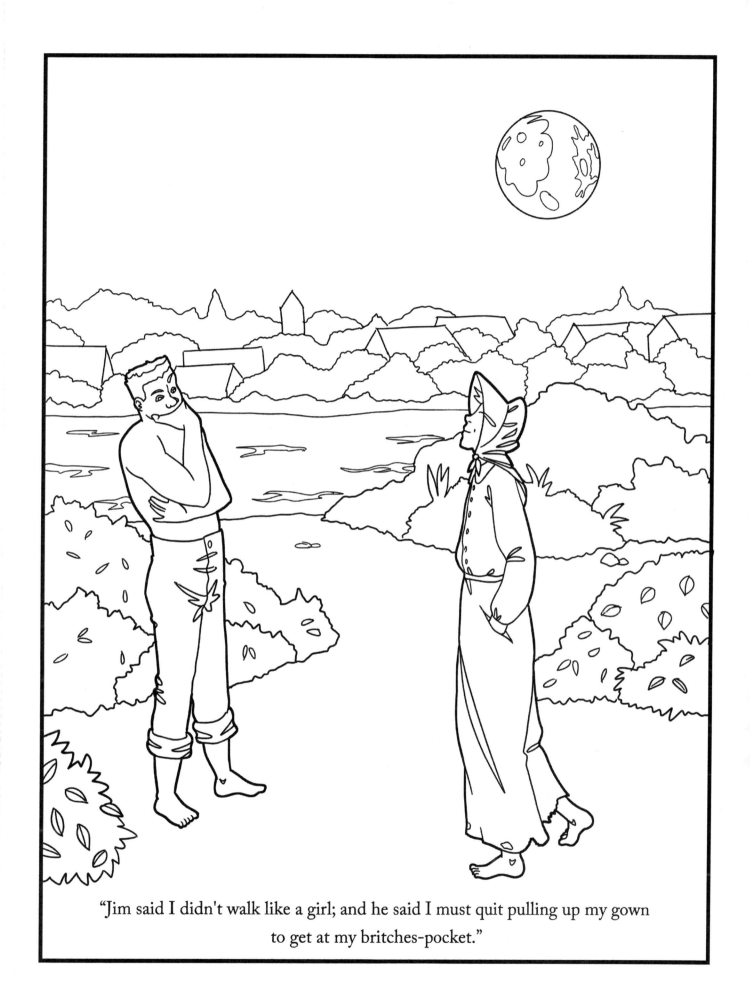

"Jim said I didn't walk like a girl; and he said I must quit pulling up my gown to get at my britches-pocket."

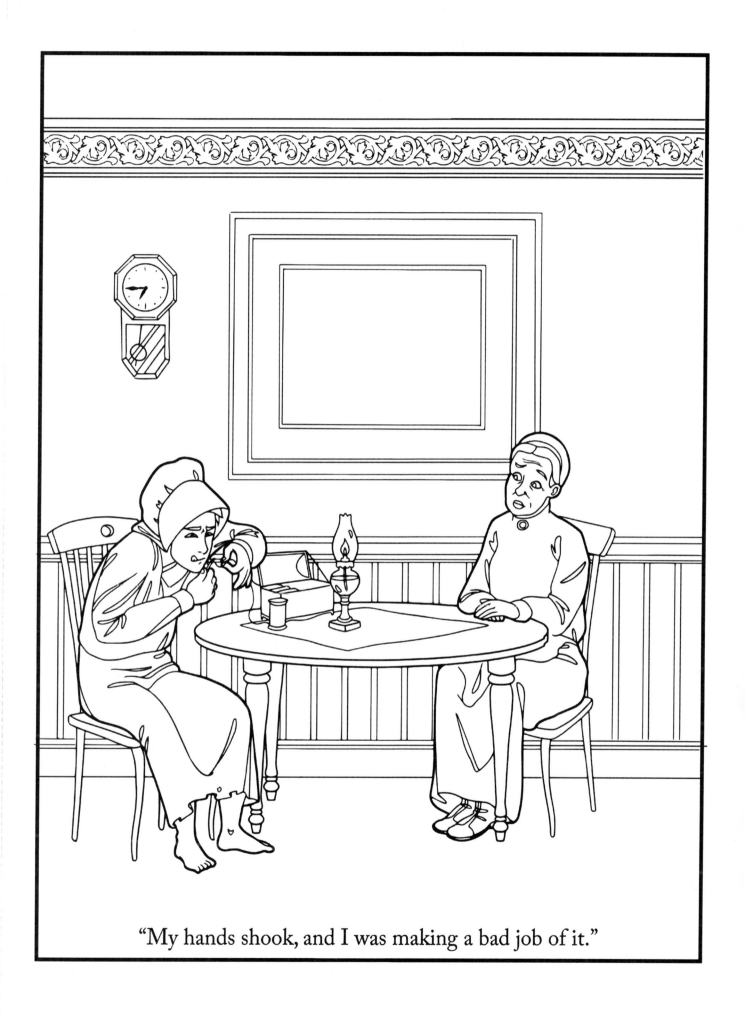

"My hands shook, and I was making a bad job of it."

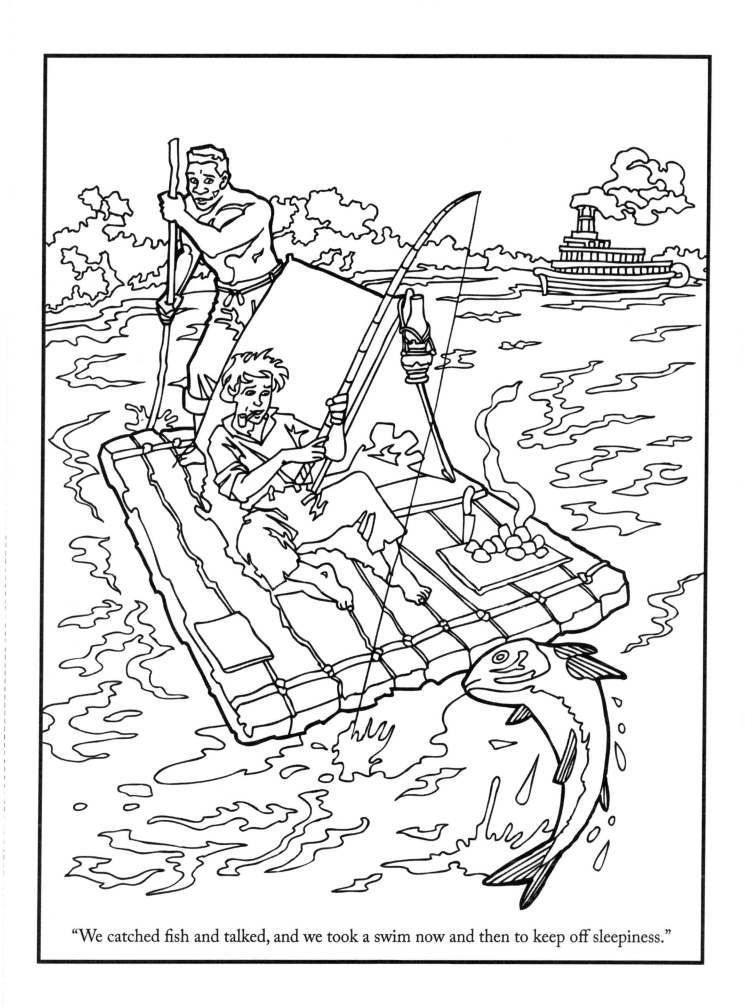

"We catched fish and talked, and we took a swim now and then to keep off sleepiness."

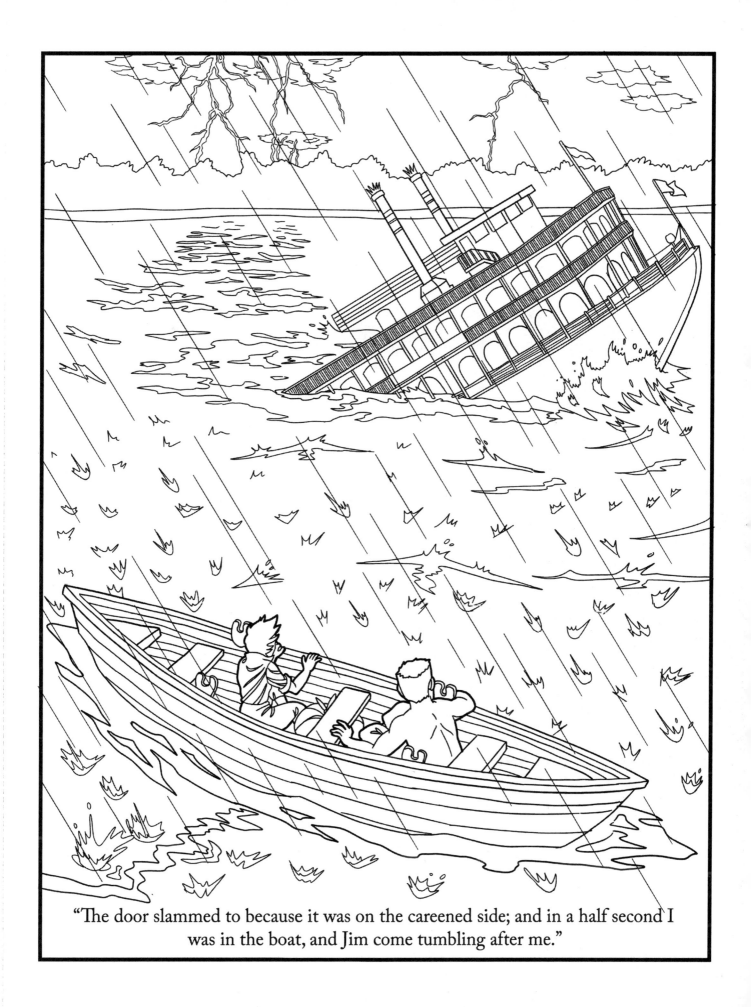

"The door slammed to because it was on the careened side; and in a half second I was in the boat, and Jim come tumbling after me."

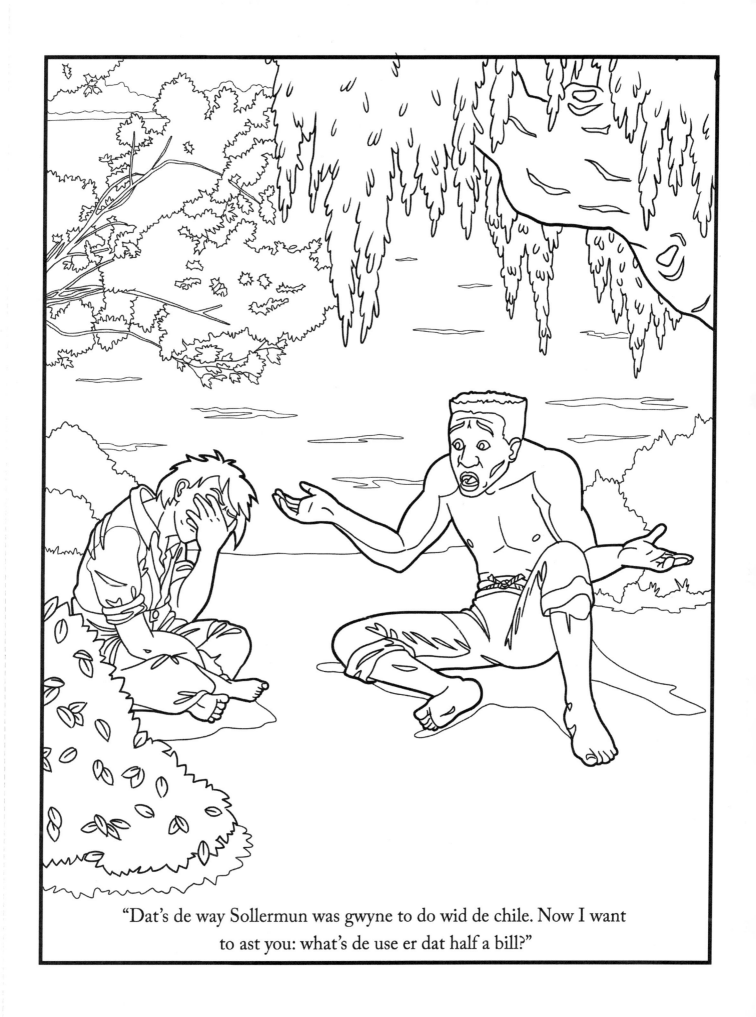

"Dat's de way Sollermun was gwyne to do wid de chile. Now I want to ast you: what's de use er dat half a bill?"

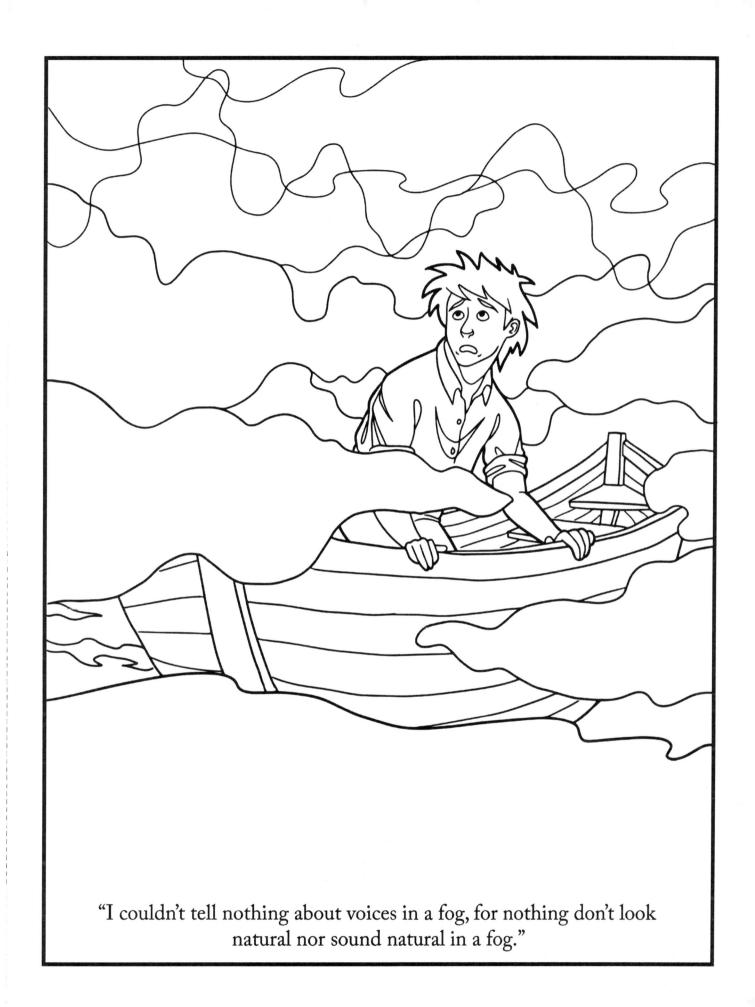

"I couldn't tell nothing about voices in a fog, for nothing don't look
natural nor sound natural in a fog."

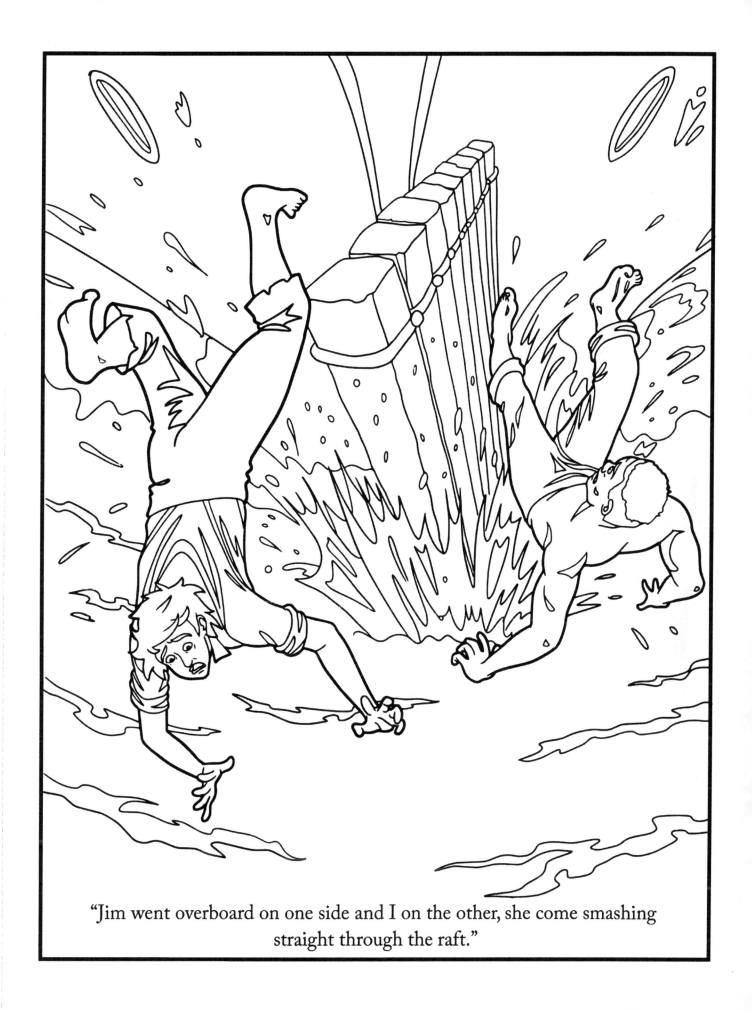

"Jim went overboard on one side and I on the other, she come smashing straight through the raft."

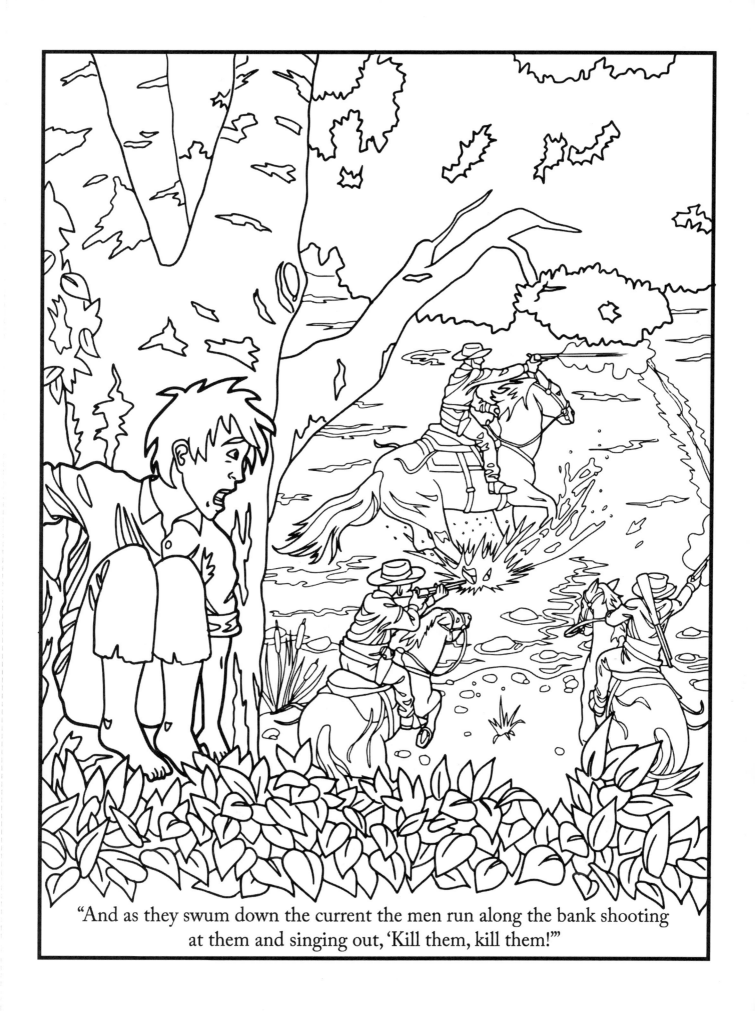

"And as they swum down the current the men run along the bank shooting at them and singing out, 'Kill them, kill them!'"

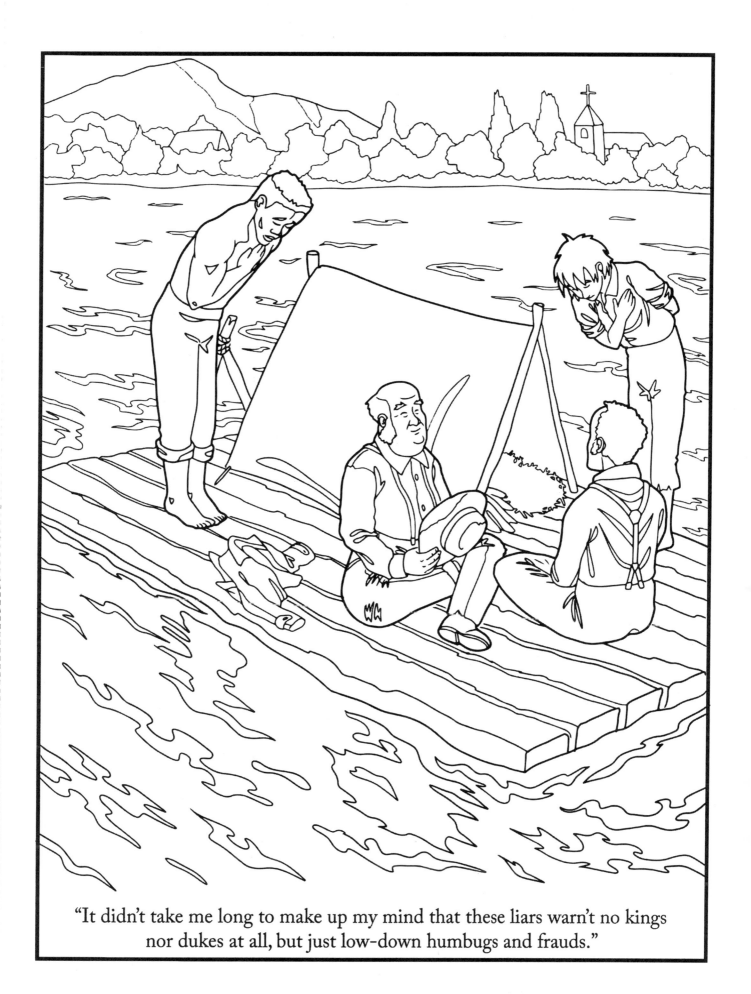

"It didn't take me long to make up my mind that these liars warn't no kings nor dukes at all, but just low-down humbugs and frauds."

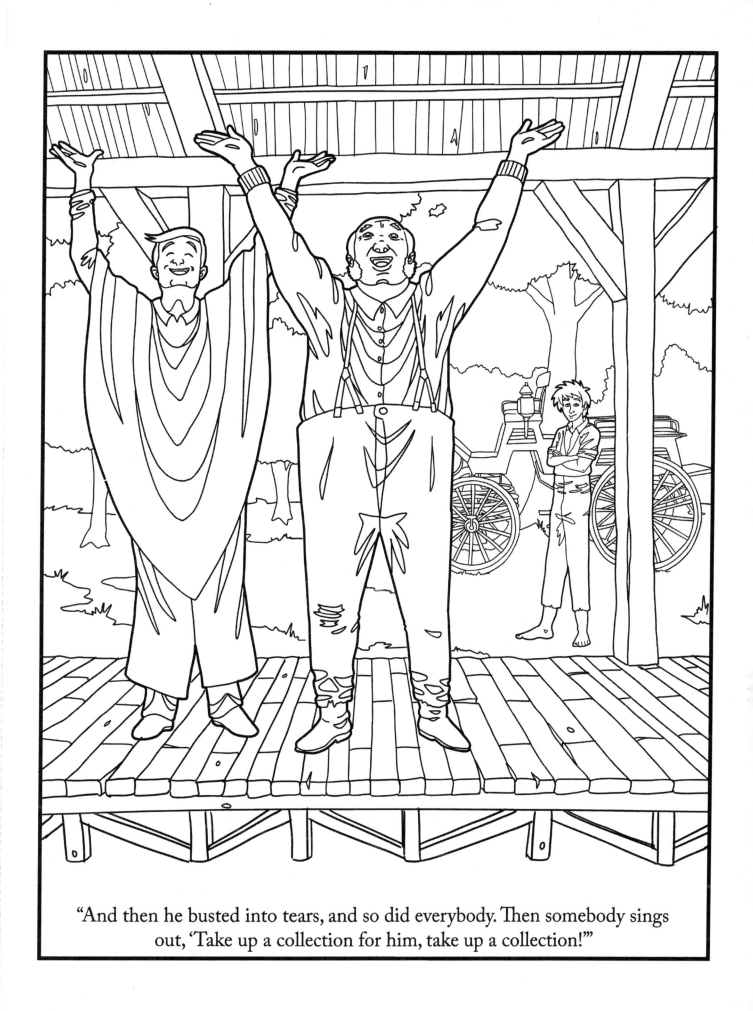

"And then he busted into tears, and so did everybody. Then somebody sings out, 'Take up a collection for him, take up a collection!'"

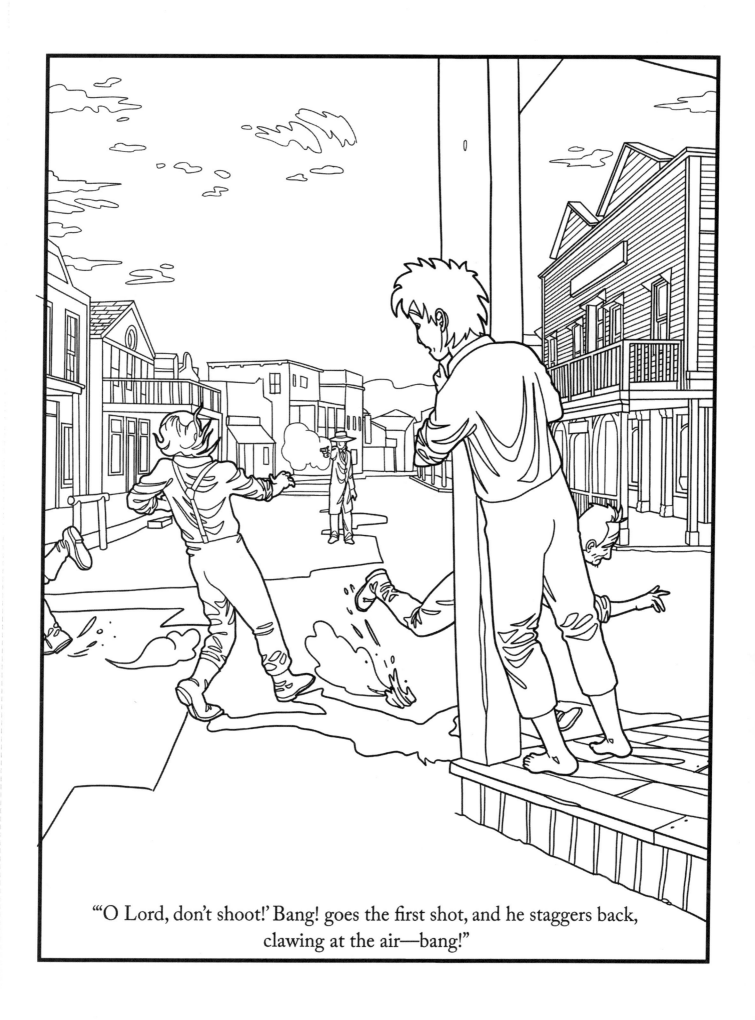

"'O Lord, don't shoot!' Bang! goes the first shot, and he staggers back, clawing at the air—bang!"

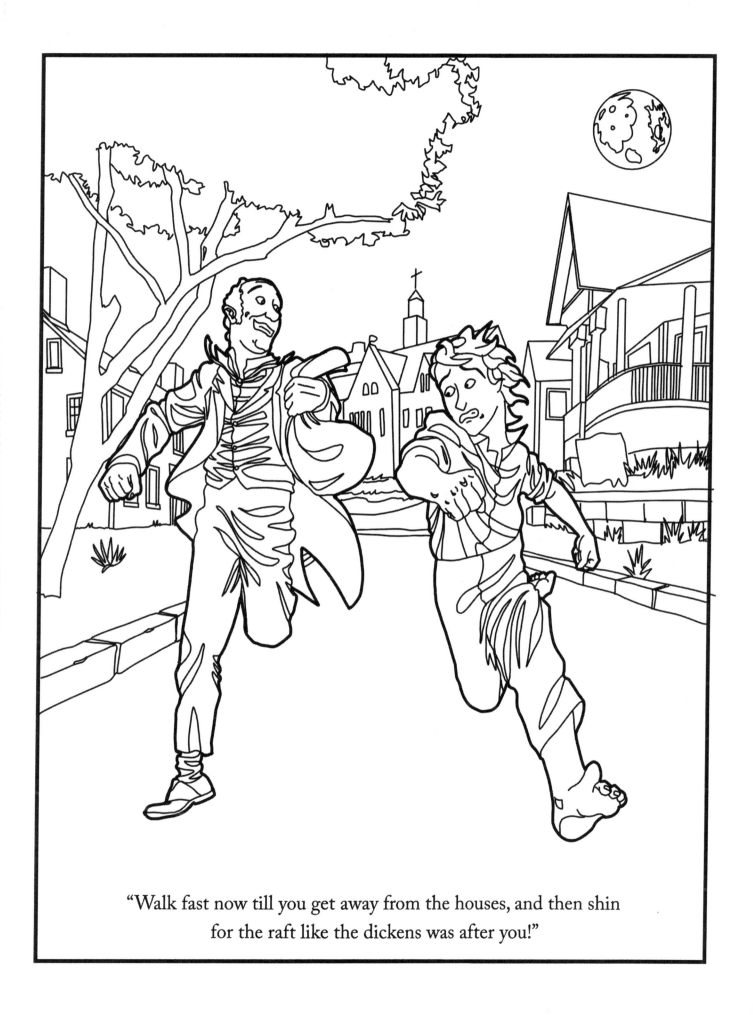

"Walk fast now till you get away from the houses, and then shin
for the raft like the dickens was after you!"

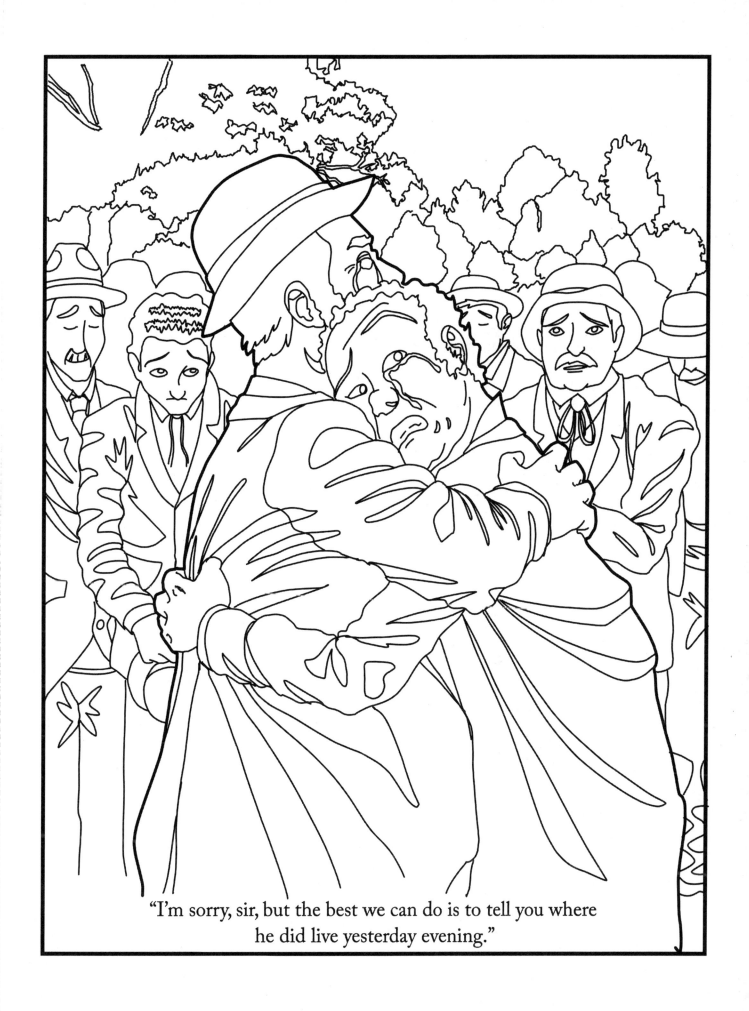

"I'm sorry, sir, but the best we can do is to tell you where
he did live yesterday evening."

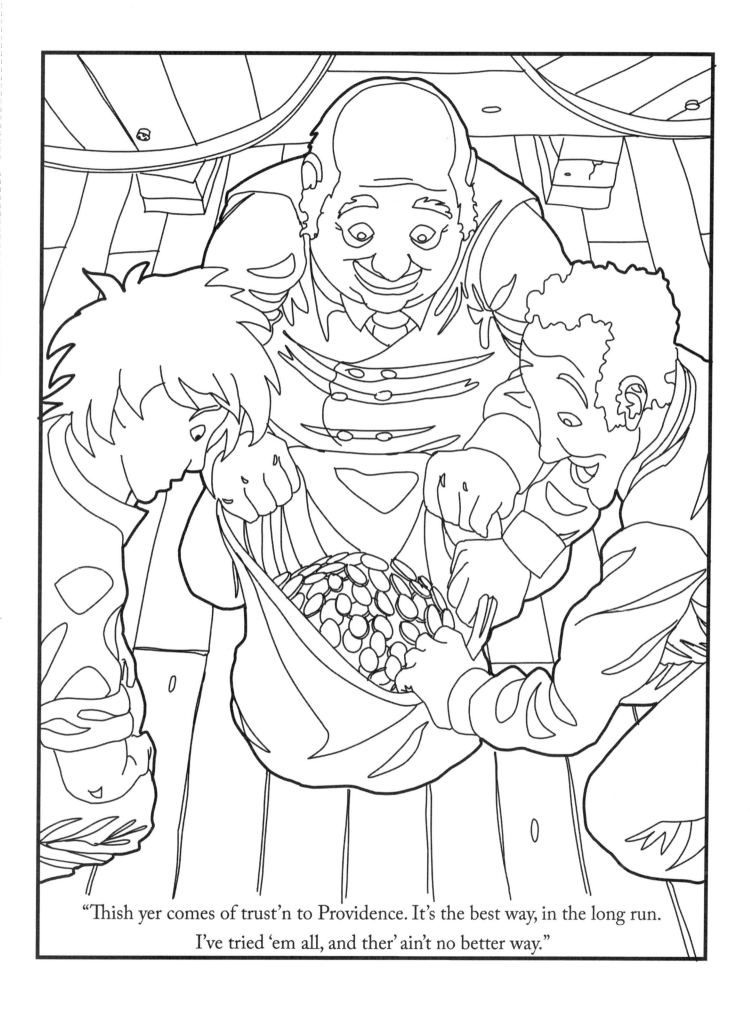

"Thish yer comes of trust'n to Providence. It's the best way, in the long run.
I've tried 'em all, and ther' ain't no better way."

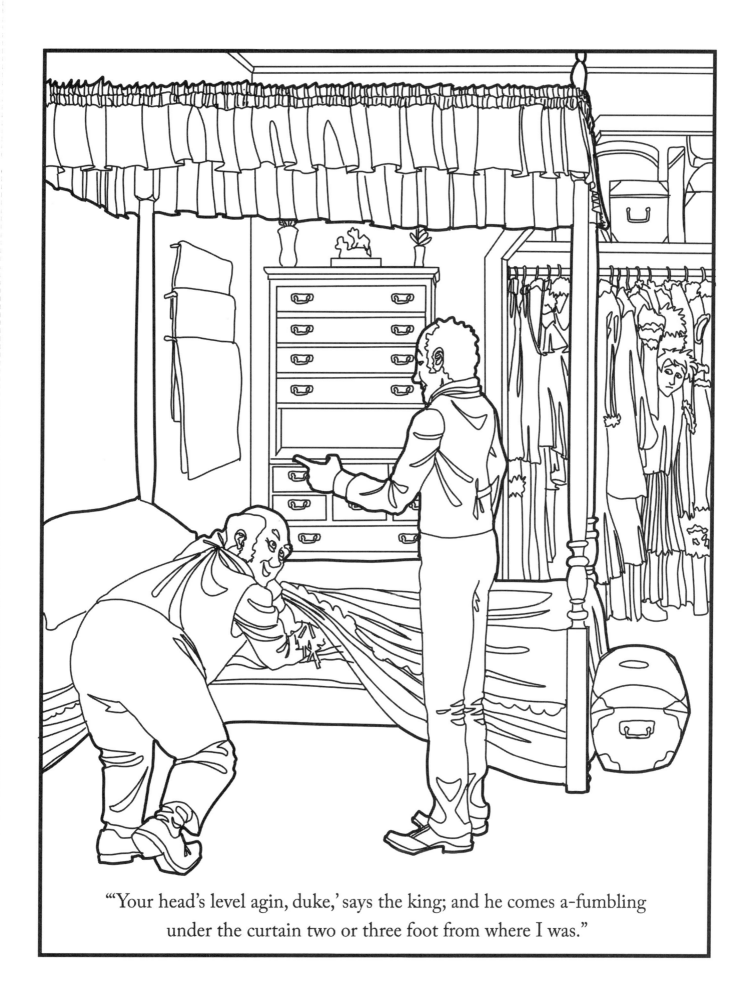

"'Your head's level agin, duke,' says the king; and he comes a-fumbling under the curtain two or three foot from where I was."

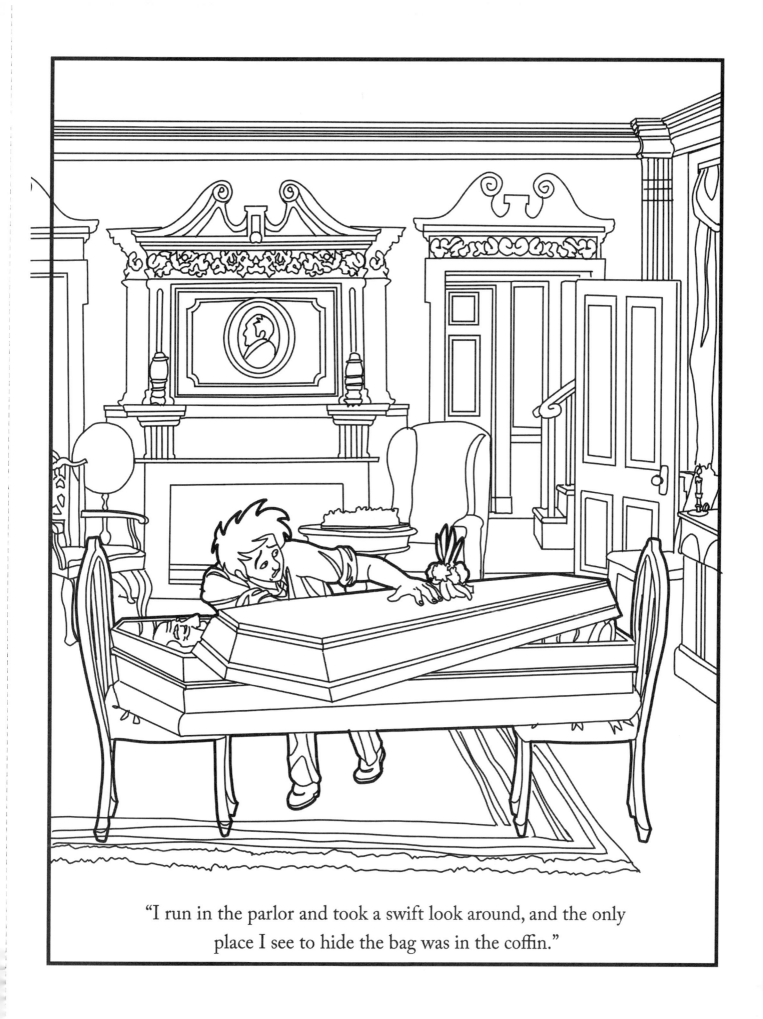

"I run in the parlor and took a swift look around, and the only
place I see to hide the bag was in the coffin."

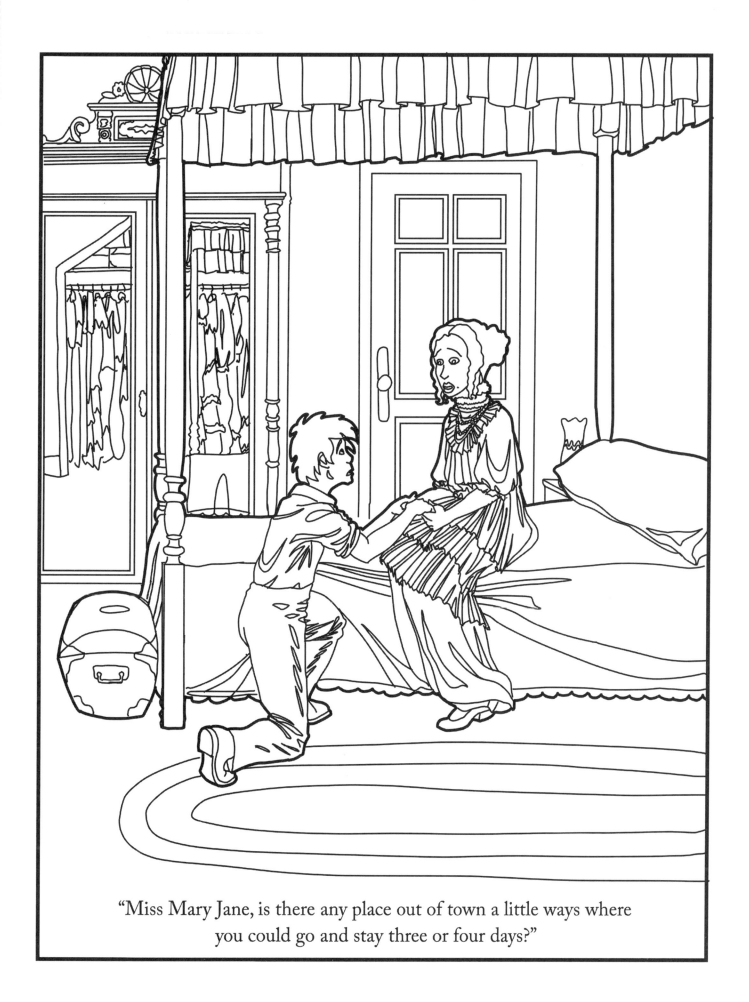

"Miss Mary Jane, is there any place out of town a little ways where
you could go and stay three or four days?"

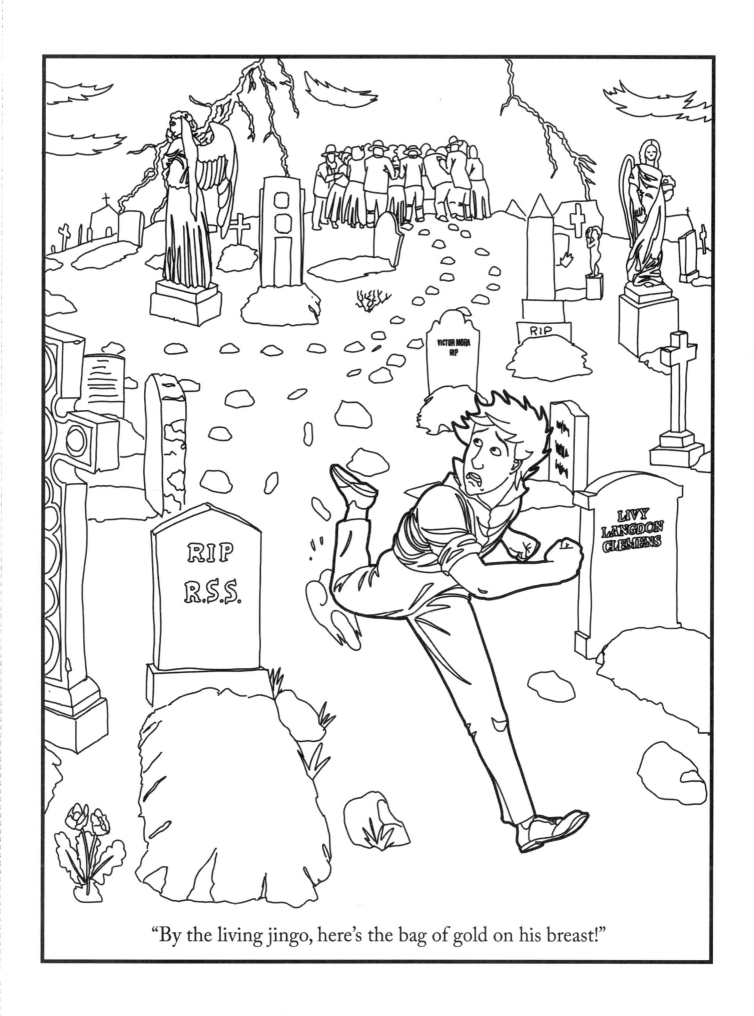

"By the living jingo, here's the bag of gold on his breast!"

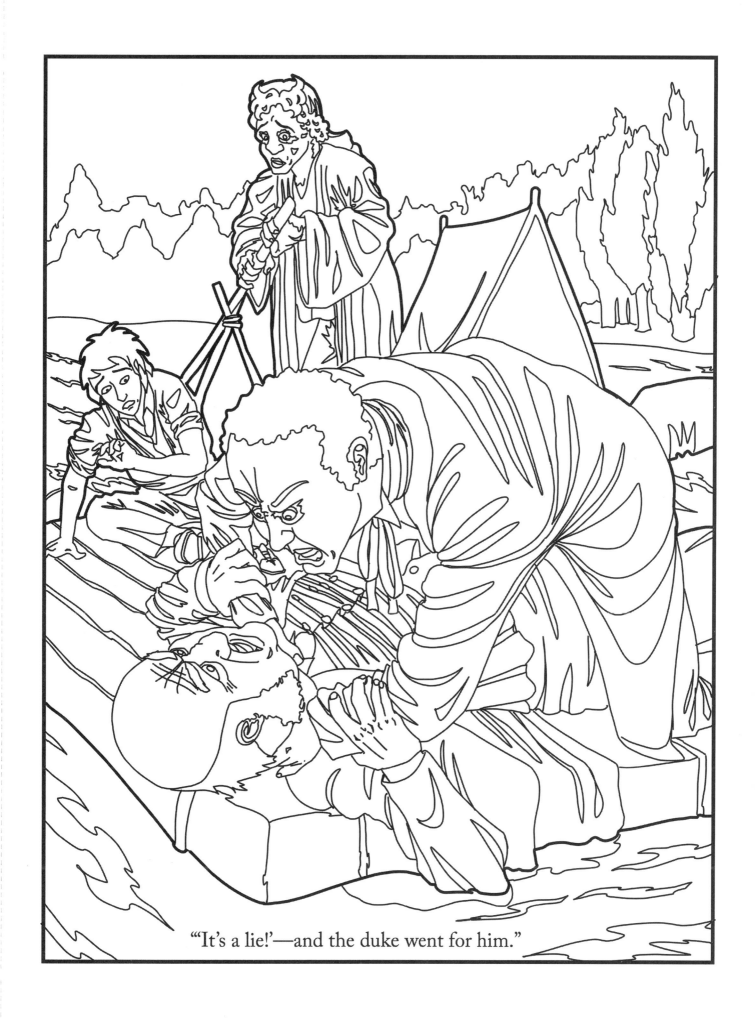

"'It's a lie!'—and the duke went for him."

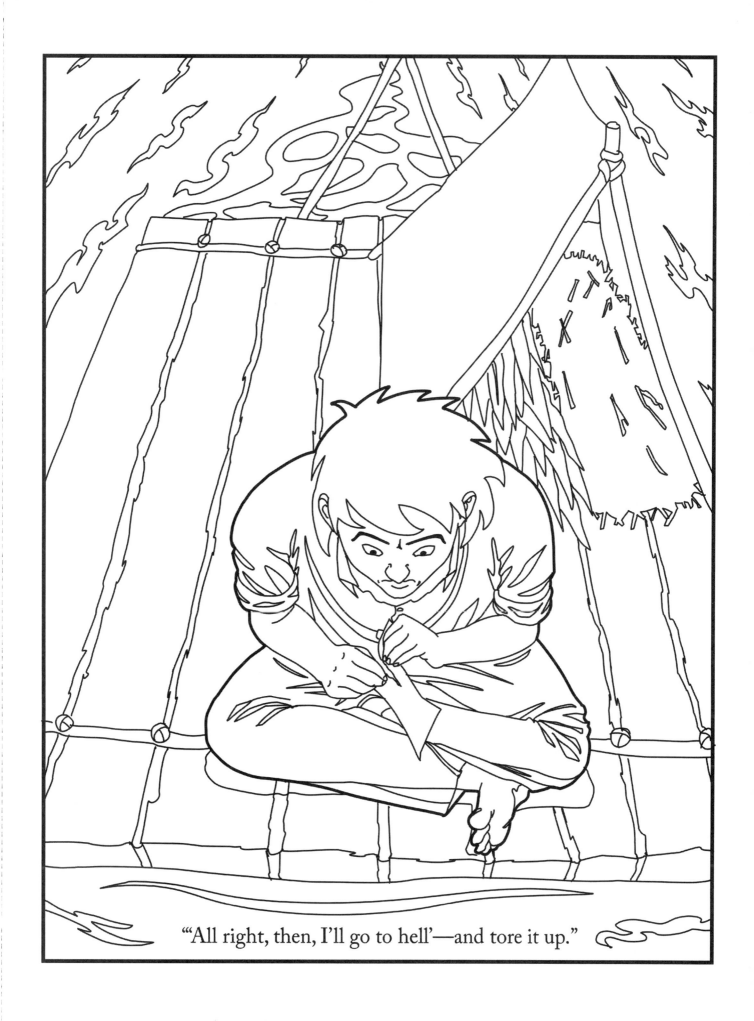

"'All right, then, I'll go to hell'—and tore it up."

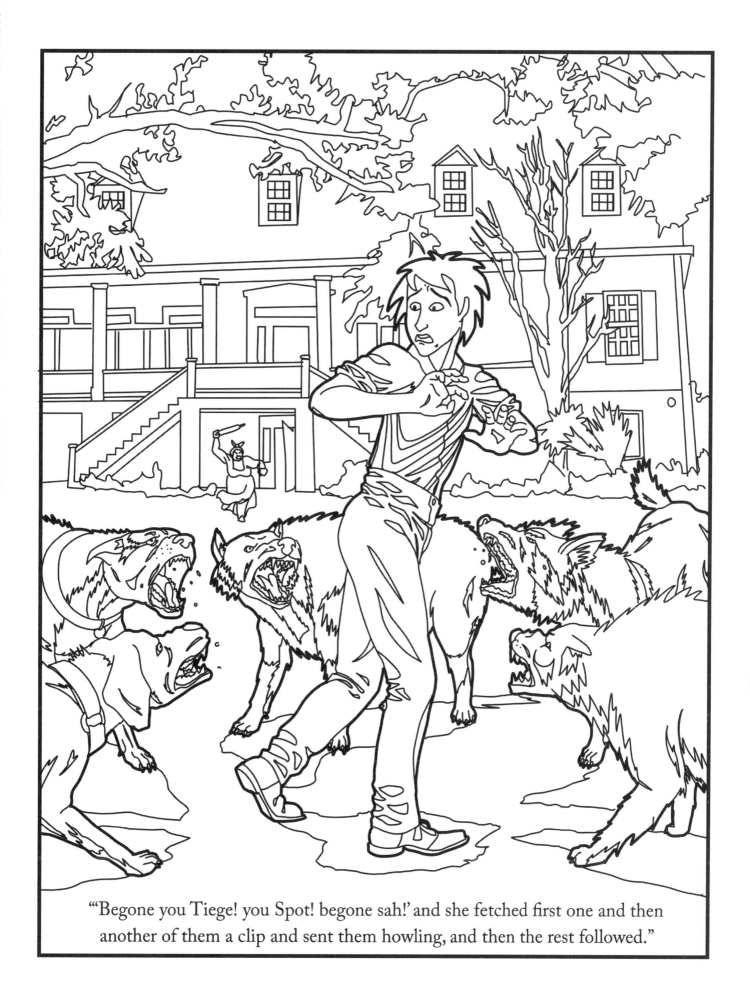

"'Begone you Tiege! you Spot! begone sah!' and she fetched first one and then another of them a clip and sent them howling, and then the rest followed."

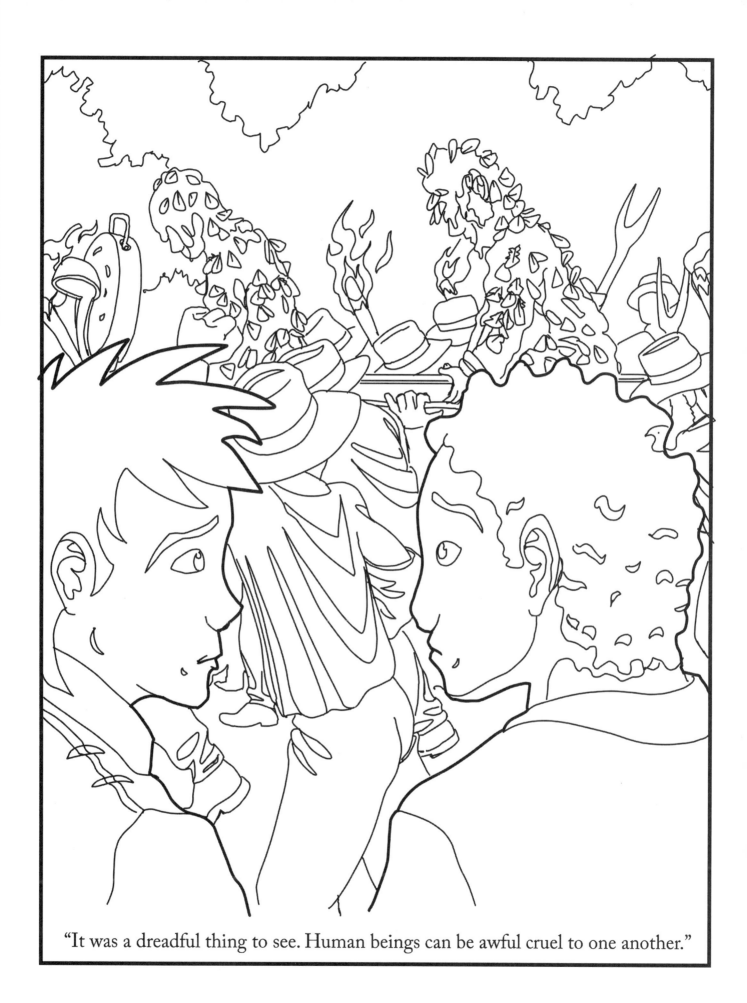

"It was a dreadful thing to see. Human beings can be awful cruel to one another."

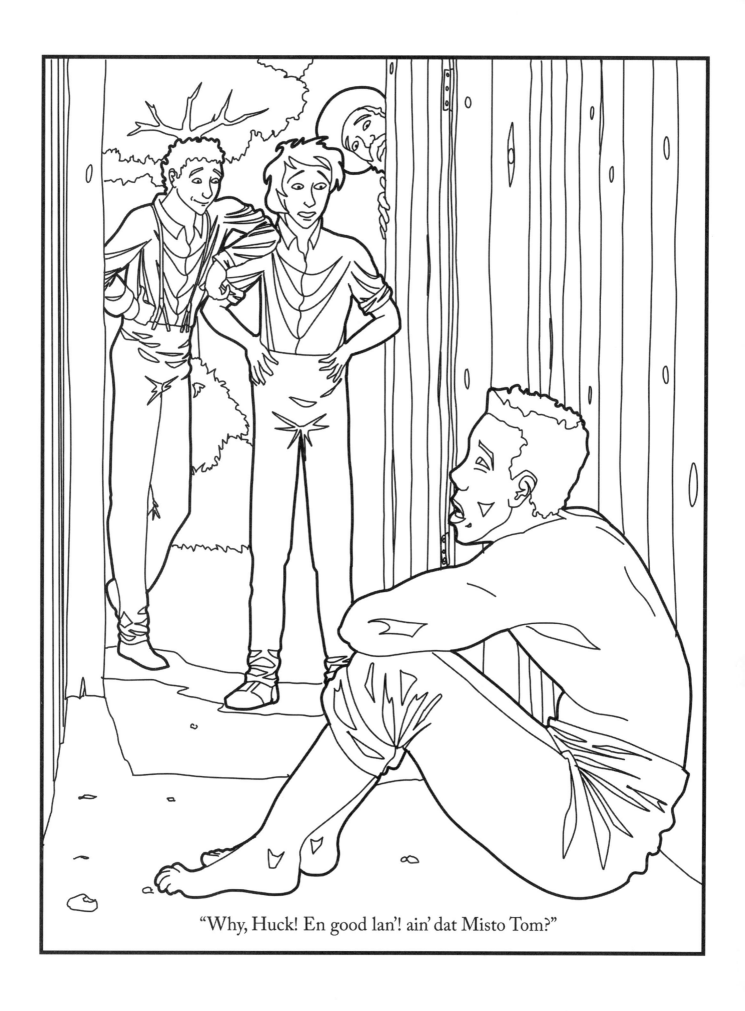

"Why, Huck! En good lan'! ain' dat Misto Tom?"

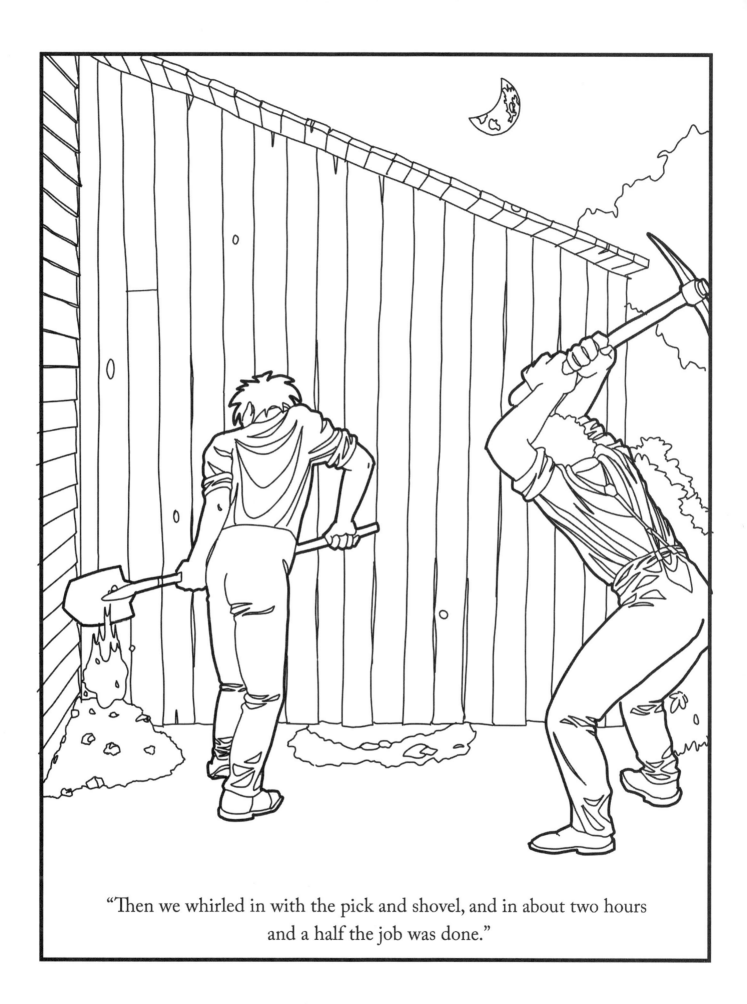

"Then we whirled in with the pick and shovel, and in about two hours and a half the job was done."

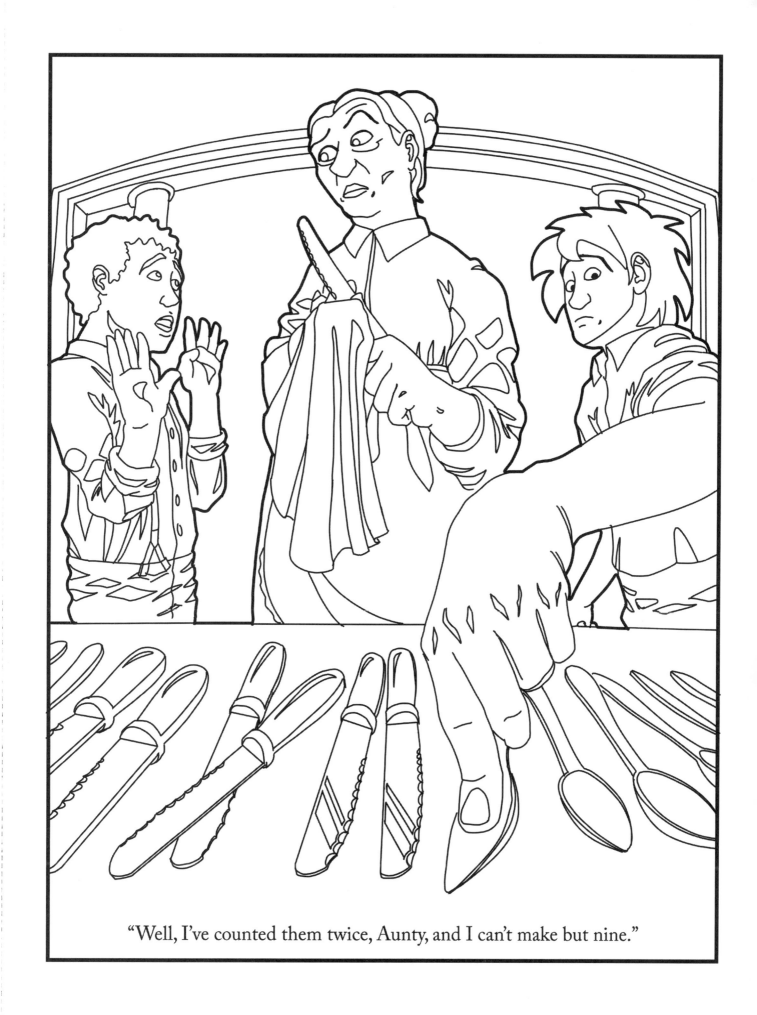

"Well, I've counted them twice, Aunty, and I can't make but nine."

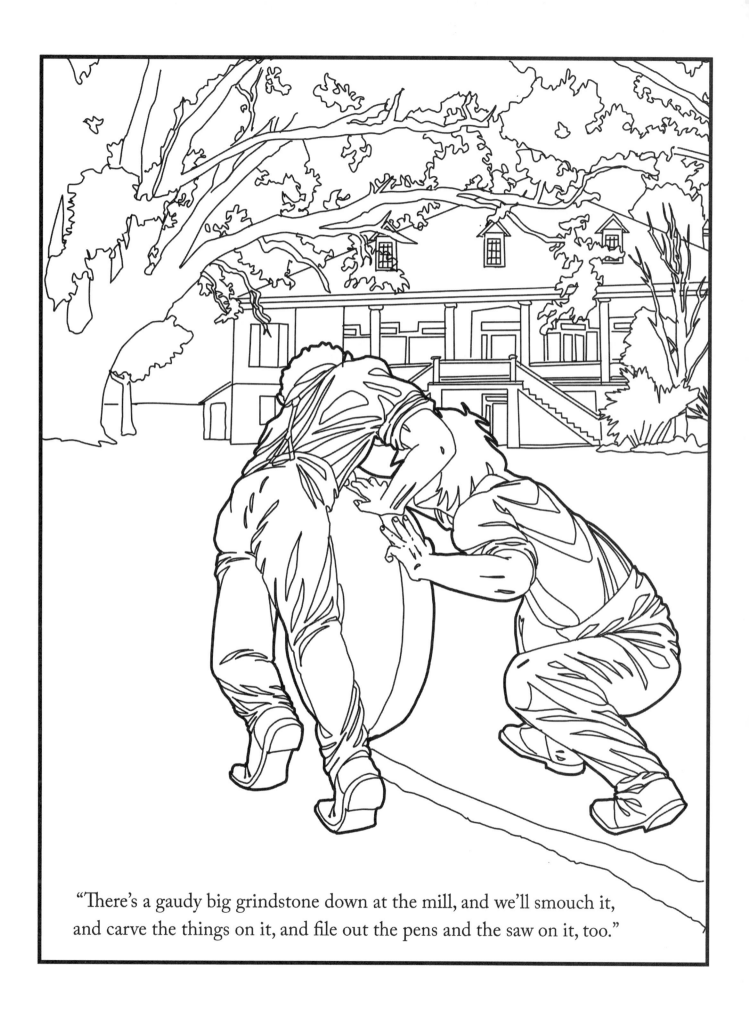

"There's a gaudy big grindstone down at the mill, and we'll smouch it, and carve the things on it, and file out the pens and the saw on it, too."

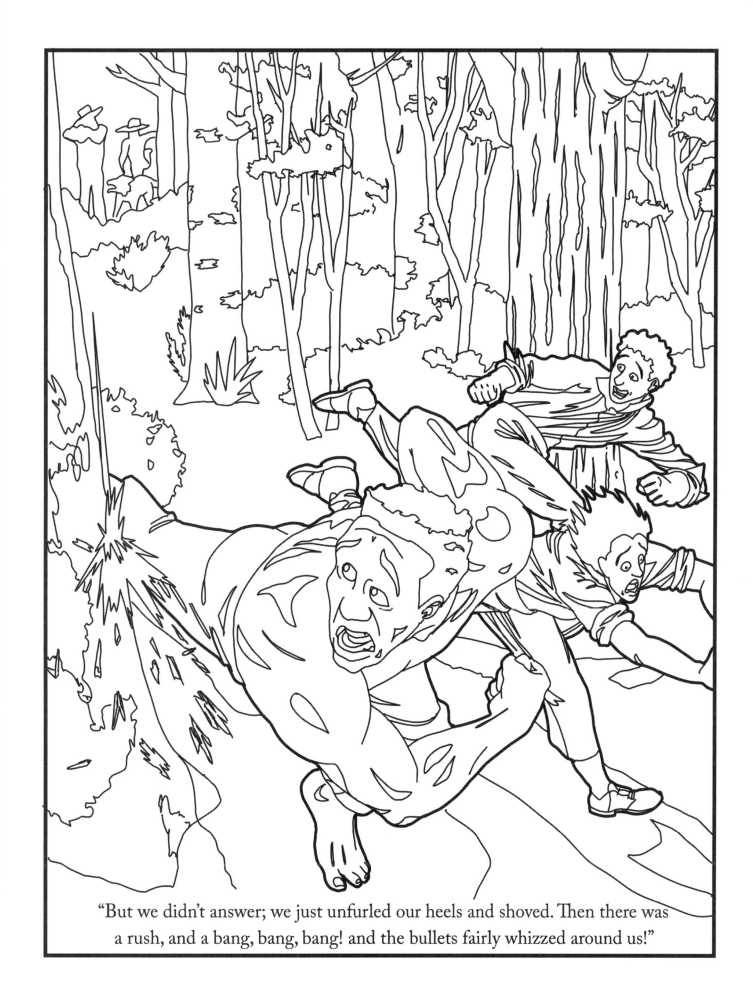

"But we didn't answer; we just unfurled our heels and shoved. Then there was a rush, and a bang, bang, bang! and the bullets fairly whizzed around us!"

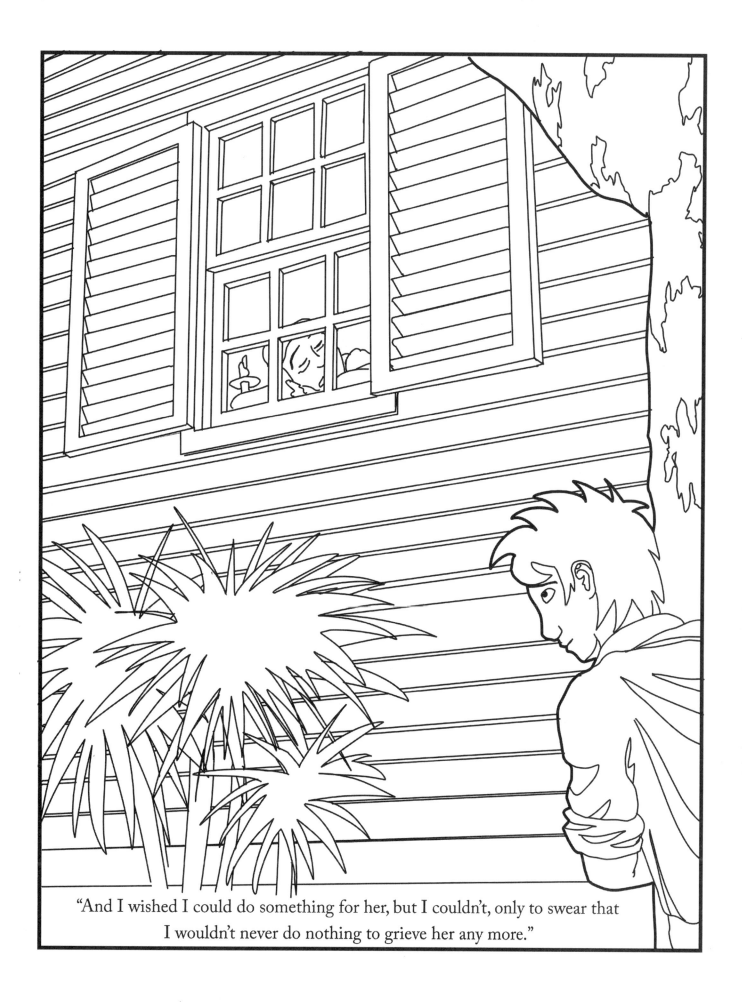

"And I wished I could do something for her, but I couldn't, only to swear that I wouldn't never do nothing to grieve her any more."

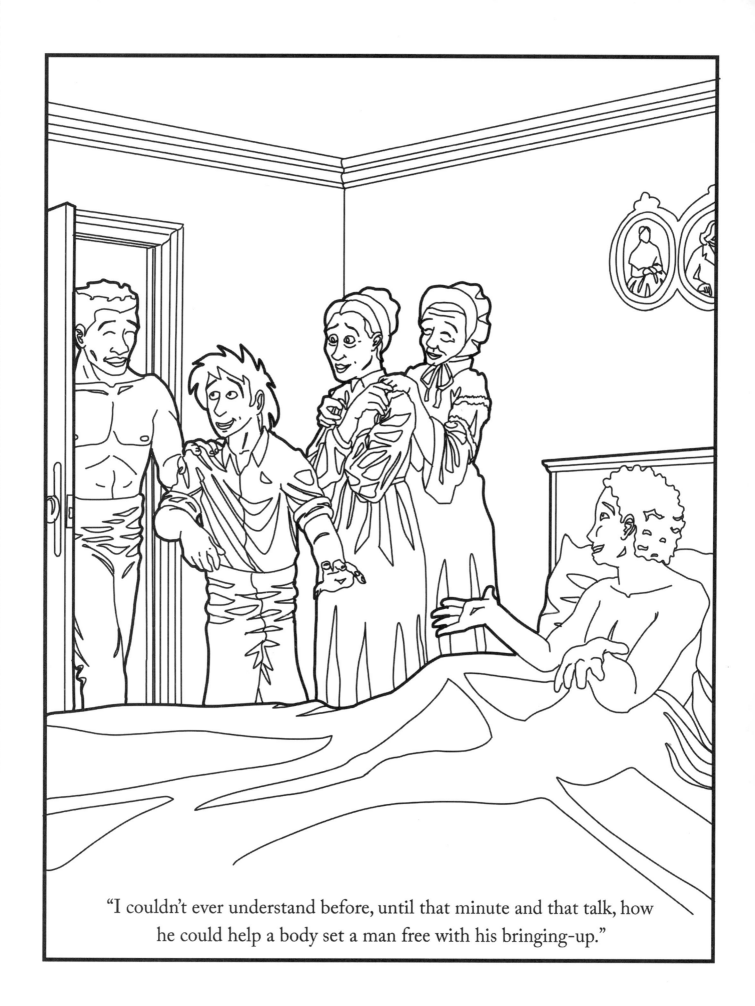

"I couldn't ever understand before, until that minute and that talk, how he could help a body set a man free with his bringing-up."